MY SISTER'S NAME IS
ROVER

Rover
Shows Off

WOOF!
WOOF!

Chris Powling and
Scoular Anderson

A & C Black • London

Rockets

ROVER - Chris Powling and Scoular Anderson

Rover's Birthday
Rover the Champion
Rover Goes to School
Rover Shows Off

First paperback edition 2000
First published 1999 in hardback by
A & C Black (Publishers) Ltd
35 Bedford Row, London WC1R 4JH

Text copyright © 1999 Chris Powling
Illustrations copyright © 1999 Scoular Anderson

The right of Chris Powling and Scoular Anderson
to be identified as author and illustrator of this work
has been asserted by them in accordance with
the Copyright, Designs and Patents Act 1988.

ISBN 0-7136-5202-0

A CIP catalogue record for this book is available
from the British Library.

Printed and bound by G. Z. Printek, Bilbao, Spain.

My sister's real name is Sara.

Nobody calls her that any more, though.
Not when she's wearing the puppy
costume Granpa made for her.

And sometimes
she adds:

This is so you don't forget.
If you do, you're in trouble.

Take this morning for example.
First the postman forgot.
He was in a hurry and wasn't
really thinking.

Rover chased him all the way to the gate.

Then the girl who delivers the
newspaper arrived.

The poor girl was so scared that she turned and ran, spilling papers and magazines everywhere.

After this, the window cleaner decided
to sort my sister out.

He tied her up tight to the
gatepost.

He reckoned she'd never undo the knot with her big, puppy paws. Soon he was singing to himself at the top of his ladder.

It only took Rover a moment to
set up the garden sprinkler.

By the time the water burst through she
was safely back by the gate.

'Rain?' said the window cleaner.
'How can it be raining on a hot
summer's day like this?'
He came down the
ladder fast.
Too fast.

There was no way he could blame my sister for the accident, though. She was snoozing in the sun with her head on her paws.

Mind you, she didn't fool grumpy Mrs Robinson who lived next door. She saw the whole thing from the kitchen window, and came rushing round to our house.

Mrs Robinson stared at Granpa.

She went back inside, slamming the back door behind her.

Still, Mrs Robinson was right about one thing. When my sister put on her puppy costume, you could rely on her to do whatever she liked. In fact she was a real show off. And whenever she got into trouble she had the perfect excuse.

It wasn't me, Barney. It was Rover.

And by that afternoon, I'd really had enough.

Honestly, when my sister's name was
Rover, she just didn't care.

The trouble was, Mum and Dad thought
she was funny.

Even Granpa wouldn't listen to me.

Granpa shrugged. 'Ask your sister.'
So I did.

All she said was:

Now if that's not showing off, what is?

I stormed off in search of some peace and quiet. But Rover wouldn't leave me alone for a second. She just followed me round the house, whining...

After a while, this really got on my nerves.

But when I complained, Mum got angry with me.

She's Rover. That's what she keeps telling us.

Mum gave me one of her looks.

Guess what?

Rover and I went walkies.

I tried to take her round the garden, but this wasn't enough for Rover. After a few laps, she leapt over the garden wall, dragging me behind her.

I ask you – a kid who's at the top of the
Juniors being pulled along by an Infant
dressed up in a puppy costume. I've
never felt such a wally in my life.

At least, I did at first. To my surprise, nobody else was bothered. Practically everyone in the village seemed to know there was a new pet in our house.

My sister really loved it. She was so good at it there were moments when I almost believed she was a proper dog myself.

When we finally got past her adoring fans, I headed for the old church. This was as far as we were allowed to go on our own.

'You can have a run here, Rover,'
I told her. 'But stay inside the churchyard.'

Probably, she didn't even hear me.

She was too busy chasing a rabbit.

Poor rabbit.

It wasn't used to dogs that yell,
'I'M GOING TO GET YOOOOO...'

34

Still, I was glad to be rid of my sister for
a while. That's assuming it wasn't a long
while, naturally. Churchyards can be
creepy places when you're alone.

Suddenly I felt the sky clouding over.
I heard the wind shifting in the trees.
I saw shadows slipping over the grass.

Then I heard voices behind me – the voices of a couple of big kids pushing bikes by the sound of it.

As I turned round they came to a halt, blocking my way.

'Rover!' I called out, hoarsely. 'Rover!'

39

Of course, they were only pretending
to be tough. I think.

They both laughed at that.

The taller one took a step towards me
and waved his arms about.

At that exact moment, my sister came
yapping back.

She was still on all fours. Her fur was dusty and bedraggled from chasing the rabbit... and she had a huge cobweb hanging from her snout.

What's more she was still showing off.

'I'M GOING TO GET YOOOOOOO...' she howled.

The two boys went goggle-eyed.

They stood there, horror struck.

At least, they did for a nanosecond.
Then they took off on their bikes
like a pair of racing cyclists.
By the time Rover had skidded
to a halt beside me, they were
almost out of sight.

My sister scratched her head with her paw. 'Who were they?' she asked.

I'd used the wrong name.

Of course, Rover paid me back for that.
As we sprinted home, she snapped and
nipped at my heels every step of the way.

The End